Against All Odds, The Resilient Coach

Navigating the Landscape of S.P.O.R.T.S.

By

Coach Dr. Kevin Wilbon Sr.

Author's Dedication

I dedicate this book to my three sons, Kevin Wilbon Jr., Kevon C. Wilbon and Christian K. Wilbon, whom I've raised, trained, and coached in all of the sports they've participated, and competed in. All three competed in Football, Basketball, Baseball, and Soccer, and I had the pleasure of being their head coach in each of those sports.

I also dedicate this book to every athlete, male or female, that I've coached or mentored over 41 years. It was a joy to meet and work with them, and some of them went on to do great things beyond sports.

To the real coaches:

Finally, I dedicate this book to what I consider the real coaches! Those are the coaches who can take an athlete to higher heights at their lowest moments, who can take a subpar athlete and coach them to where their progression sets in. That can take an athlete who never played a sport but was interested in it and make them formidable. Any coach can inherit athletic talent, sharpen their skills, and get recognition as a great coach, but can they take someone who has no talent and turn them around to be a competitive foe? Those are the coaches who should be recognized. People say winning isn't everything; well, I feel that coaches who give their time, talent, and commitment in coaching to any athlete in any sport and caring about them are everything!

Acknowledgment

I would like to acknowledge the realest and sincerest coaches that I've had the pleasure to either coach with, compete against, or to ever meet. Especially those who share the visions and core values of S.P.O.R.T.S., such as I have.

Coach Gerald Moore Jr.,

Dr. Bill Price,

Coach David Barmer

Coach Brian Walker,

Coach Marvin Bennett Sr.,

Coach Adano Murray,

Coach David McGlone,

Coach Stan Holloway (Olympics Track Star Grant Holloway's dad)

Coach William Marshall,

Coach Darrell Gardner,

Coach William Drakeford Sr.

Coach Charles Oliver (CoachO)

Coach Andrew Dutrow

Coach Henry McCallum

Author'sz Bio

Born on November 22, 1961, and raised in the urban parts of Washington DC, Coach Dr. Kevin Wilbon Sr. is one of six siblings. He is a retired US Army Military Veteran of twenty-four years, and his areas of expertise were Logistics, Arms Room Weapons NCOIC, Contracting, Transportation NCOIC, Central Issuing Facility NCOIC, Army Drug and Alcohol Prevention and Control (ADAPC).

Coach Dr. Kevin Wilbon Sr. is an alumnus of Central Texas College of Killen, Texas, National-Louis University of Chicago, Illinois, Touro University of Callamee, California, and the North Central University of Scottsdale, Arizona. He holds five educational degrees: an Associates of Arts, a Bachelor of Science, and Masters in Education, an Master's in Business (MBA) and a Doctorate of Education Educational Leadership.

Coach Dr. Wilbon has been inducted into six prestigious Honor Societies for his educational accomplishments. His 4.0 GPA Honor Societies are the

National Society for Black Engineers, the National Society for Collegiate Scholars, the National Society of Leadership and Success, the Golden Key International Honor Society, the Kappa Delta Pi Society for Educational Leaders, and Strathmore's Professional Who's Who Honors and Awards.

His success doesn't end here; owning a love for achievements, Coach Dr. Wilbon made his way to becoming a High School Varsity Basketball coach for Boys and Girls, enjoying the success in capturing three Boys Maryland State Basketball Championships along with a Boys Maryland State Track and Field Championship, and a couple of Christian Private School Varsity Boys and Girls Basketball Championships. In his tenure as Head Coach and Assistant Coach, three dozen of his players became Division One basketball players, as well as a few of those who ended up as NBA and NFL players.

Coach Dr. Wilbon is currently the high school and middle school Head Track and Field Coach for the Southern Maryland Christian Academy in White Plains, Maryland and the head track and field coach for the Lake DC Track Club which is a part of the AAU and USATF Organizations. He is certified in several areas of sports and has been for over forty years. His certifications includes the National Federal High School, Maryland, and Virginia, certified in coaching and officiating basketball and track and field, certified in National Youth Sports Coaches Alliance Level 1,2,3 and 4, and USATF and AAU certified official and basketball coach.

Amongst his many achievements, Coach Dr. Wilbon has coached well over a thousand kids and made his way to becoming the founder and CEO of Wilbon Basketball Incorporation (WBI). WBI trains kids from ages six to eighteen in the fundamentals of basketball and track. Coach Dr. Wilbon is also a member of a Gospel singing group called the Committed Sons, led by his brother-in-law, Rodney Roach. Coach Dr. Wilbon has held over fifteen lobs in his life starting from the age of thirteen.

Not only that, but Coach Dr. Wilbon is also a proud member of the Ark of Safety Christian Church in Upper Marlboro, Maryland, headed by Bishop C.

Muse and First Lady Pat Lawson Muse, where he is on the Usher Board, Choir Board, and in the Church Drama Club headed by President/CEO and up and coming actor, director, writer, and visionary Dennis Jones.

Coach Dr. Kevin Wilbon Sr. is an Athletic Coach, Author, Military Veteran, Educator, Motivational Speaker, and Mentor. He is also an author of four books. My Observation of Bullying in the Middle Schools a Very Serious and Problematic Situation, Overcoming Bullying and It's Effects, What's your Motivation? A guide to Educational Motivation, and My Life Journey: Challenges and Triumphs from DC to DR.

Table of Contents

CHAPTER 1

S – STRATEGIZING

Dr. Wilbon's journey started right in the heart of Washington, DC, where the streets bustled with city life. Born into a bustling household with five siblings, his early years were a mix of both challenges and bravery. Growing up in the city posed its own difficulties for Coach Dr. Wilbon and his family. They had to maneuver through the crowded streets and make do with limited space and resources. Despite these obstacles, there was a strong sense of togetherness within their crowded home. In the midst of the chaos, they found unity and support among each other. It was this sense of unity and determination that helped them weather the storms of urban life and emerge stronger together. Through the ups and downs, Dr. Wilbon's family stood by each other, facing each challenge with determination and courage.

As Coach Dr. Wilbon fondly reminisces about his childhood, memories flood his mind like colorful snapshots from the past. He recalls the warmth of his crowded living room, where laughter echoed off the walls as he and his siblings engaged in playful games of hide-and-seek and tag. Despite the limited space, their home was filled with boundless energy and joy, creating a sanctuary of happiness amidst the bustling city outside. Evenings were a time for family gatherings, with raucous family dinners around the dinner table becoming a cherished tradition. The aroma of home-cooked meals filled the air as they shared stories and laughter, creating memories that would last a lifetime. These simple yet precious moments of togetherness were the cornerstone of Dr. Wilbon's early years, shaping his values and nurturing his sense of belonging within his family.

However, alongside the laughter, there were also moments of struggle and adversity that colored Dr. Wilbon's upbringing. The weight of financial constraints bore heavily on his family, casting a shadow of uncertainty over their daily lives. There were times when putting food on the table became a challenge, and the future seemed uncertain. Yet, it was during these difficult times that Dr. Wilbon's resilience began to take root. Despite the hardships, his family remained united, drawing strength from each other's support and determination. They found solace in the simple pleasures of life, cherishing moments of warmth and love throughout the adversity. It was through these trials that Coach Dr. Wilbon learned the value of perseverance and indomitability, lessons that would shape his character and guide him through the challenges that lay ahead.

From a young age, Coach Dr. Wilbon absorbed the significance of strategizing like a sponge soaking up water. It became clear to him that this skill would be like a trusty compass guiding him through life's tumultuous waters. Whether it was figuring out how to stretch their meager resources to cover basic needs or brainstorming creative solutions to overcome daunting challenges, Coach Dr. Wilbon tackled each obstacle with unwavering determination. Like a master chess player contemplating their next move, he meticulously planned his steps, weighing the pros and cons before taking action. His strategic approach wasn't just about finding a quick fix; it was about laying the groundwork for long-term success. With each hurdle he cleared, Dr. Wilbon's confidence in his ability to aviate life's twists and turns grew stronger, cementing strategizing as his greatest ally in the face of adversity.

One of Dr. Wilbon's most cherished memories transports him back to his youthful days spent on the basketball court. It was here, amidst the bouncing of basketballs and the shouts of players, that he first discovered the profound importance of strategic thinking. Despite his tender age, Coach Dr. Wilbon quickly realized that triumphing in basketball wasn't solely reliant on raw talent and skill; it demanded a keen intellect and astute planning. As he dribbled the ball across the court, his mind buzzed with calculations and observations, analyzing his opponents' movements and discerning patterns that could be exploited to gain an advantage.

With each match, Dr. Wilbon's strategic acumen grew sharper, like a blade honed by constant use. He meticulously studied his adversaries, scrutinizing their playing styles and tendencies with the precision of a seasoned detective unraveling a mystery. Armed with this knowledge, he crafted intricate plays and maneuvers, coordinating with his teammates to outwit their opponents and secure victory on the court. It wasn't just about scoring points; it was about outmaneuvering the opposition, employing strategy and teamwork to emerge triumphant.

Through countless hours of practice and dedication, Coach Dr. Wilbon honed his ability to think several moves ahead, anticipating his opponents' actions and devising counterstrategies to thwart their advances. His time on the basketball court became a crucible for the development of his strategic prowess, instilling in him a profound appreciation for the power of foresight and planning in achieving success. As he reflects on those formative years, Coach Dr. Wilbon realizes that the lessons learned on the basketball court transcend the confines of the game, permeating every aspect of his life and shaping his approach to overcoming obstacles and seizing opportunities.

Dr. Wilbon's journey through basketball exemplifies the transformative impact of strategic thinking, demonstrating how a young enthusiast with a passion for the game evolved into a strategic mastermind capable of sailing across life's challenges with finesse and determination.

But strategizing wasn't merely a skill reserved for the basketball court; it was a guiding principle that infiltrated every facet of Dr. Wilbon's life, shaping his approach to challenges both big and small. From traversing the labyrinthine corridors of the education system to navigating the turbulent waters of personal adversity, Coach Dr. Wilbon applied his strategic mindset with unwavering determination.

Reflecting on his journey, Coach Dr. Wilbon comes to a profound realization: strategizing transcends mere planning—it's a mindset, a way of life. It's about embracing challenges as opportunities for growth and finding innovative solutions when faced with obstacles. It's about maintaining a steadfast focus on the end goal, even when faced with seemingly insurmountable odds.

In the face of adversity, Dr. Wilbon's strategic approach served as a beacon of hope, guiding him through the darkest of times. Whether it was devising a plan to overcome financial hardships or negotiating the complexities of personal relationships, he remained steadfast in his commitment to strategic thinking. And time and time again, it was this unwavering resolve that allowed him to triumph over adversity and emerge stronger on the other side.

As Dr. Wilbon's journey demonstrates, strategizing isn't just a tool for achieving success—it's a way of life. It's about embracing challenges head-on, armed with a clear goal and a well-thought-out plan. And with each hurdle cleared, Dr. Wilbon's belief in the power of strategic thinking only grew stronger, solidifying its place as his greatest asset in the journey of life.

Coach Dr. Wilbon shares his stories to help us discover ourselves and feel stronger. He shows us that no matter how hard things get, we can overcome them with valor, determination, and smart thinking. As we face life's challenges, Coach Dr. Wilbon reminds us that having a good plan can make all the difference. He encourages us to believe that we have the power to succeed, even when things seem tough. Dr. Wilbon's words give us hope and remind us that we can achieve anything if we stay strong and think smart. So, as we read his stories, we feel inspired to tackle our own challenges and grow stronger along the way.

CHAPTER 2

P – PROGRESSING

In the heart of bustling Washington, DC, young Wilbon and his family faced unique challenges amidst the city's vast landscape. Living in a cramped home with scarce resources, they tackled the intricacies of urban living with creativity and resolve. Despite the tight quarters, their bond grew stronger as they weathered the hustle and bustle of city life together. In the midst of the crowded streets and bustling activity, Wilbon and his siblings found solace in each other's company, forming deep connections that would endure the tests of time. Their shared experiences forged a sense of unity and camaraderie, providing a source of strength and support in the face of adversity. Together, they navigated the complexities of city life, relying on one another's ingenuity and determination to overcome obstacles along the way. Despite the challenges they faced, their tight-knit family remained a beacon of resilience and hope amidst the urban sprawl of the nation's capital.

As time went by, Dr. Wilbon's life journey continued, showing his unstoppable drive to move forward and get better. Even when he faced challenges, he never gave up on his quest for success. Whether he was studying in the respected halls of schools or serving in the tough military, Coach Dr. Wilbon grabbed every chance to learn and grow. His life story showed how resilience and determination could change everything, proving that with steady dedication and effort, great things could happen.

Dr. Wilbon's journey wasn't easy, but it was filled with valuable lessons. Each obstacle he encountered only made him stronger and more determined to succeed. He learned that setbacks were just opportunities to learn and grow, pushing him to become better with each challenge he faced. From academic achievements to military service, Dr. Wilbon's journey was a shining example of what could be achieved with perseverance and hard work. Through his unwavering dedication, Coach Dr. Wilbon showed that anything was possible if you were willing to put in the effort and never give up on your dreams.

Dr. Wilbon's journey wasn't just about school and the military; it was also about his deep love for basketball. Ever since he was young, basketball filled him with excitement and passion. Playing on the court gave him a thrilling feeling, and coaching and guiding young players brought him immense happiness. Basketball wasn't just a game for Dr. Wilbon; it was a big part of his life's journey.

On the basketball court, Coach Dr. Wilbon experienced a mix of emotions. There were moments of exhilaration when he scored points and helped his team win games. But there were also tough times when his team faced challenges and losses. Through it all, he learned valuable lessons about teamwork, discipline, and leadership. He discovered that working together with teammates was essential to success, and staying disciplined helped him improve his skills. As he transitioned from player to coach, Coach Dr. Wilbon found joy in mentoring young athletes, guiding them through their own journeys on and off the court.

Apart from the excitement of playing basketball, Coach Dr. Wilbon gained valuable lessons that helped him in life. He discovered the importance of talking openly, solving problems, and not giving up when things got tough. These lessons weren't just for the basketball court; they influenced how Coach Dr. Wilbon dealt with challenges in everyday life. Basketball became a teacher for Dr. Wilbon, guiding him through personal growth and development. It taught him to stay determined and resilient, qualities that became his strengths in facing various situations. The experiences he had while playing basketball shaped his character and prepared him for whatever life threw his way. Whether it was facing challenges at work, dealing with personal issues, or pursuing his goals, Dr. Wilbon's lessons from basketball were always there to guide him.

Looking back on his life, Coach Dr. Wilbon sees how much growth and learning influenced his journey toward success. He understands that his ability to keep going despite challenges made a big difference. Dr. Wilbon's story shows how determination and a strong desire to improve can lead to great things. It's a story about not giving up, no matter what obstacles come your way.

Coach Dr. Wilbon wants his story to encourage others to keep growing and striving for their dreams. He knows that everyone has the potential to achieve greatness if they're willing to put in the effort. Through his experiences, Coach Dr. Wilbon hopes to show others that they can overcome any challenge with determination and perseverance. He wants to inspire them to seize every opportunity for growth and never lose sight of their goals.

Dr. Wilbon's journey is a reminder that success isn't just about talent or luck; it's about hard work and resilience. He believes that by sharing his story, he can help others see that they have the power to shape their own destinies. Dr. Wilbon's message is one of hope and empowerment, encouraging others to believe in themselves and their ability to achieve their dreams.

CHAPTER 3

O – OBSTACLES

Dr. Wilbon's childhood home in bustling Washington, DC, was a lively place, constantly buzzing with activity. With a big family and visitors dropping by frequently, the house was always brimming with people. Sometimes, it seemed like there wasn't even enough space to stretch out comfortably. In the neighborhood where Coach Dr. Wilbon lived, challenges were as common as the bustling streets.

Money was often scarce, making life tough for Coach Dr. Wilbon and his family. They had to stretch every dollar to make ends meet, and sometimes even the basics felt like luxuries. Buying groceries or paying bills became a balancing act, with every penny carefully accounted for. Despite the hardships, Dr.

Wilbon's family held onto hope and worked hard to navigate through the tough times.

Living in such a dynamic environment taught Coach Dr. Wilbon valuable lessons about resilience and perseverance. He learned to appreciate the little joys amidst the chaos and to find strength in the support of his loved ones. These early struggles laid the foundation for his determination to overcome obstacles and chase his dreams, no matter how daunting they seemed.

Coach Dr. Wilbon had a strong determination burning inside him like a bright flame. Even when life threw its toughest challenges at him, he never lost sight of his dreams. He had big plans for himself - he wanted to do really well in school and land a good job in the future. No matter how hard things got, Coach Dr. Wilbon held onto his dreams tightly, like treasures worth protecting.

School days weren't always smooth sailing for Coach Dr. Wilbon. Sometimes, it felt like he was wandering in a confusing maze, unsure of which path to take. But he refused to let the maze defeat him. Instead, he rolled up his sleeves and got to work. Whenever he stumbled upon a dead-end or a tricky turn, he wasn't afraid to ask for help. Slowly but surely, with each step forward, Coach Dr. Wilbon began to unravel the mysteries of the education system.

It wasn't always easy. There were times when he felt like giving up, like throwing in the towel and calling it quits. But Coach Dr. Wilbon had a fire burning inside him, a relentless determination that refused to be extinguished. He knew that giving up wasn't an option if he wanted to achieve his dreams. So, he pressed on, one step at a time, determined to carve a path for himself despite the obstacles that stood in his way.

Joining the military was like stepping into a whole new world for Dr. Wilbon. It was tough, with days stretching out long and the work never seeming to end. But Coach Dr. Wilbon didn't let the daunting challenges scare him away. Even when things didn't go according to plan, he refused to throw in the towel. Instead, he dug his heels in deeper and kept marching forward.

In the military, Coach Dr. Wilbon learned firsthand the importance of adaptability. When faced with obstacles, he realized that sticking to the same old tactics wouldn't always work. Sometimes, he had to think on his feet and change his approach to overcome the hurdles in his path. It wasn't easy, but Coach Dr. Wilbon embraced the challenge, knowing that it was the key to survival.

Sports played a significant role in Dr. Wilbon's life, offering both joy and challenges. But with the thrill of competition came the risk of injuries and the pressure of tough adversaries. There were moments when it felt like the odds were stacked against him like he was fighting an uphill battle. Yet, Coach Dr. Wilbon refused to back down. He gritted his teeth through the pain and persevered, drawing strength from his determination to succeed.

Through his experiences in sports, Coach Dr. Wilbon learned valuable lessons about resilience and perseverance. Each setback became an opportunity for growth, teaching him how to bounce back stronger than before. With every hurdle he cleared, Coach Dr. Wilbon emerged more resilient, more determined, and more prepared to tackle whatever challenges lay ahead.

Coaching was like stepping into a whole new ball game for Dr. Wilbon. It wasn't just about knowing the ins and outs of the sport; it was also about managing a whole team of players, each with their own personalities and quirks. At times, it felt like trying to corral a group of unruly cats! But Coach Dr. Wilbon didn't let the chaos overwhelm him.

Instead, he rolled up his sleeves and dove headfirst into the challenge. He learned how to navigate the dynamic world of team dynamics, finding ways to bring out the best in each player while fostering a sense of unity among them. It wasn't always smooth sailing. There were disagreements, conflicts, and moments of frustration. But Coach Dr. Wilbon remained steadfast, always keeping his eyes on the ultimate goal.

Through the ups and downs of coaching, Coach Dr. Wilbon gained valuable insights into the importance of resilience. He learned that setbacks were just part of the game and that success often required bouncing back from failures with even more determination than before. He also learned the value of adaptability, understanding that sometimes, the playbook needed to be rewritten in order to overcome new challenges.

With each game won and lost, Coach Dr. Wilbon grew stronger and more capable. He became not just a coach but a mentor and a leader, inspiring his team to push past their limits and reach for greatness. In the end, it was these lessons in resilience and adaptability that propelled Coach Dr. Wilbon to victory, both on and off the field.

One of the most crucial lessons Coach Dr. Wilbon learned along his journey is that you don't have to tackle obstacles all by yourself. It's perfectly okay to reach out for support when you need it. Whether it's a listening ear from a friend, a comforting hug from family, or wise advice from a mentor, there are always people around who are ready and willing to lend a helping hand.

Dr. Wilbon's own experiences are a shining example of this truth. Whenever he encountered a roadblock or felt overwhelmed by the challenges ahead, he didn't hesitate to seek assistance. He leaned on his loved ones for encouragement and guidance, drawing strength from their unwavering support.

Through the ups and downs, Coach Dr. Wilbon discovered that having a support network made all the difference. It gave him the courage to keep moving forward, even when the path seemed uncertain. And with each step he took, he realized that no obstacle was insurmountable as long as he had people to lean on and share the burden with.

Dr. Wilbon's journey stands as a testament to the power of determination, resilience, and the support of others. It proves that with a strong will and a little help from those around you, there's no challenge too great to overcome. So, if you're facing difficulties in your own life, take heart in Dr. Wilbon's example. Don't give up. Keep pushing forward, and eventually, you'll break through the barriers and reach your goals, just like Coach Dr. Wilbon did.

CHAPTER 4

R—RESILIENCE

Resilience is indeed like a superpower—a secret strength that helps you stand tall even when life throws its toughest punches. Dr. Wilbon's journey is a testament to the incredible power of resilience. Growing up amidst the hustle and bustle of Washington, DC, Coach Dr. Wilbon encountered numerous challenges that could have easily knocked him down. But instead of letting these obstacles defeat him, he used them as stepping stones to rise higher.

Life in urban Washington, DC, was no walk in the park for Dr. Wilbon. In a neighborhood where difficulties seemed to lurk around every corner, he faced hardships that would make many others crumble. Money was tight, and opportunities were scarce. But instead of succumbing to despair, Coach Dr. Wilbon turned each challenge into an opportunity for growth.

With each hurdle he faced, Coach Dr. Wilbon discovered new depths of resilience within himself. Every setback, whether it was struggling in school or facing hardships at home, became a lesson in perseverance. He refused to let adversity define him, instead choosing to rise above it with unwavering determination.

As Coach Dr. Wilbon navigated the twists and turns of his life journey, his resilience only grew stronger. Joining the military was a daunting challenge, but he faced it head-on, drawing on his inner resilience to conquer the obstacles in his path. Even when faced with setbacks and unexpected twists, Coach Dr. Wilbon refused to be deterred. He learned to adapt and overcome, using his resilience as a shield against life's adversities.

Through it all, Coach Dr. Wilbon's resilience remained his most potent weapon. It was the driving force that propelled him forward, even when the road ahead seemed daunting. In the end, it was this resilience that allowed him to overcome every obstacle and emerge victorious, inspiring others to do the same along the way.

Life in bustling urban Washington, DC, posed numerous challenges for young Dr. Wilbon. His neighborhood seemed like a place where difficulties lurked around every corner, making each day a test of resilience. With limited finances and few opportunities, life often felt like an uphill battle for Coach Dr. Wilbon and his family. However, he possessed a spirit that refused to be subdued by tough circumstances.

Despite the daunting odds, Coach Dr. Wilbon chose not to let the tough conditions dictate his fate. Instead, he transformed each obstacle into a stepping stone for personal growth. Every challenge he encountered became an opportunity to fortify his resilience and determination.

Even from a tender age, Coach Dr. Wilbon understood the vital importance of resilience. With each setback he faced, whether it was struggling to keep up in school or enduring hardships within his household, he refused to yield. Instead, he confronted each obstacle head-on, viewing them as a chance to showcase his strength and perseverance.

Dr. Wilbon's unwavering resolve in the face of adversity serves as a powerful example of resilience. Rather than allowing tough circumstances to dictate his destiny, he embraced each challenge as an opportunity to thrive. Through his experiences, Coach Dr. Wilbon learned invaluable lessons about the significance of resilience, lessons that would shape his approach to life's challenges in the years to come.

As Coach Dr. Wilbon matured, his resilience blossomed into a powerful force within him. When he decided to join the military, it felt like stepping into a vast unknown, filled with challenges and uncertainties. Yet, armed with courage and determination, Coach Dr. Wilbon faced this daunting challenge head-on. Even when things didn't unfold as he had hoped, he refused to succumb to defeat. Instead, he embraced the obstacles that came his way, using his resilience as a shield to deflect the blows of adversity.

Sports played a pivotal role in shaping Coach Dr. Wilbon's resilience. On the basketball court, he encountered formidable opponents and experienced heart-wrenching losses. However, with each defeat, Coach Dr. Wilbon emerged not weakened but strengthened. He learned to turn setbacks into opportunities for growth, refusing to be discouraged by temporary failures. Every stumble became a stepping stone, propelling him forward with renewed determination.

The basketball court became a battleground where Coach Dr. Wilbon honed his resilience skills. Each game tested his perseverance and mental fortitude. Despite the challenges, Coach Dr. Wilbon never wavered in his commitment to success. He understood that resilience wasn't just about bouncing back from defeats; it was about maintaining unwavering resolve in the face of adversity.

Through his experiences in sports, Coach Dr. Wilbon learned invaluable lessons that transcended the confines of the basketball court. He discovered the true essence of resilience - the ability to endure hardships and emerge stronger on the other side. Dr. Wilbon's journey serves as a testament to the transformative power of resilience, showing that with determination and perseverance, even the toughest challenges can be overcome.

Coaching and mentoring weren't just roles Coach Dr. Wilbon took on; they became natural extensions of his own resilience. Drawing from his personal experiences, he used his journey as a source of inspiration and guidance for others. Whether it was a struggling athlete grappling with setbacks or a troubled youth navigating difficult circumstances, Coach Dr. Wilbon offered a helping hand and words of encouragement.

Through his coaching and mentoring, Coach Dr. Wilbon shared stories of resilience in action, illustrating how he overcame various challenges in his life. From conquering injuries that threatened to derail his dreams to facing personal hardships that tested his resolve, Coach Dr. Wilbon showcased the transformative power of resilience. His aim was not only to share his own triumphs but also to instill hope and motivation in others, showing them that resilience is a force capable of overcoming even the toughest adversities.

By opening up about his journey, Coach Dr. Wilbon aimed to ignite a spark of resilience in the hearts of his readers. He wanted them to understand that resilience isn't just about avoiding failure altogether—it's about finding the strength to rise up each time life knocks you down. Through determination, courage, and a steadfast commitment to never giving up, Coach Dr. Wilbon proved that any obstacle could be overcome.

So, for those grappling with challenges in their own lives, Dr. Wilbon's story serves as a beacon of hope and inspiration. It reminds us that resilience isn't an elusive trait reserved for the select few—it's a quality that lies within each of us, waiting to be cultivated and nurtured. With Coach Dr. Wilbon as a guiding example, readers are encouraged to embrace their inner resilience and press forward with renewed determination, knowing that they, too, have the power to overcome any obstacle and achieve their dreams.

****

Roosevelt Jamauri Cunningham, the 3rd, fondly known as Roosevelt, embarked on a journey that defied expectations and showcased the power of determination and resilience. Born as a vibrant and active baby, Roosevelt's early years were marked by a struggle with speech delay and mild autism. Despite these challenges, his parents remained steadfast in their commitment to his well-being, seeking specialized speech therapy to aid in his communication development. Additionally, upon discovering his mild autism, his parents resolved to provide unwavering support and care for him throughout his life.

At the age of six, Roosevelt's father witnessed a remarkable display of determination and strength when he found his son carrying a 30-pound bag of dog food with determination and perseverance. This pivotal moment spurred Roosevelt's father to introduce him to the world of sports, initially through football. Despite showing promise as a quick and strong player, Roosevelt's football journey was short-lived due to concerns about potential injuries.

However, fate had a different plan for Roosevelt when, at the age of seven, his father introduced him to basketball. In a serendipitous moment at a local park, Roosevelt effortlessly sunk five consecutive shots during his first encounter with a basketball, igniting a newfound passion for the sport. Recognizing Roosevelt's natural talent and affinity for basketball, his father provided him with opportunities to hone his skills, including installing a basketball hoop in their backyard.

Intrigued by his son's burgeoning talent and dedication, Roosevelt's father sought out Dr. Coach Wilbon to further nurture Roosevelt's basketball skills. Under Dr. Coach Wilbon's guidance, Roosevelt underwent rigorous training and development in fundamental basketball techniques, quickly progressing from a novice to a formidable player. With unwavering support from his family and dedicated coaching, Roosevelt flourished on the basketball court, transitioning from a second-string player to a pivotal member of his team.

Roosevelt's talent and work ethic did not go unnoticed, as he led his team to an undefeated season and secured a championship victory. His success continued to soar as he advanced through countywide basketball and AAU leagues, garnering attention from collegiate scouts and receiving offers from various schools. Despite his remarkable achievements, Roosevelt remained humble and dedicated to his team, earning praise from teammates and coaches alike for his selflessness and sportsmanship.

Throughout his basketball journey, Roosevelt defied stereotypes and surpassed expectations, proving that with determination, resilience, and unwavering support, anything is possible. His story serves as an inspiration to all, highlighting the transformative power of sports in overcoming challenges and achieving greatness.

ROOSEVELT CUNNINGHAM

COACH DR. WILBON WITH ROOSEVELT DURING A TRAINING SESSION

ROOSEVELT CUNNINGHAM DUNKING THE BASKETBALL

Another strong case of resilience is attributed to my son Christian Wilbon who will becoming a high school senior at Westlake High School in Waldorf Maryland. He has a couple of collegiate goals and aspirations, he's going to pursue a degree in law and to major in theater as a minor. What makes him a great candidate and asset to any school and track team is the fact that he's academically proficient, and his grades are great as well. He pays attention to detail in any task that is handed down to him, whether academically or athletically. He considers himself a leader but is always willing to learn and go beyond what is expected of him. He's been an honorable student since elementary school. Christian hit a major bump in the road dealing with injuries and growth spurts around 12 years old. He was used to being on top and being one of the best track runners his age in the State of Maryland and the country.

The injuries plagued him for a while, and he was contemplating just stopping running track for good. I told him that injuries are a setback but part of the game and he has to be mentally and physically strong to succeed to mount a comeback, but the desire has to come from the heart as well as the mind. Christian opted to do physical rehabilitation and focus on the positive narrative because he loved the sport. This was tough and draining on his body. As he moved along, he slowly but surely was making progress, although once he got back on the track he wasn't winning right away. He would lose races to kids that he used to dominate, and this was new to him and frustrating, but he had to take it one race at a time. He had several people taunt him, make jokes, and even laugh at him. I made him go out of his comfort zone to run events he wouldn't normally run to help him get his stamina and strength back, like the 1500 meters and 5000 meters. This helped him get back closer to where he was before becoming injured. I explained to him that hard work, sacrifice, and determination are the keys to success, so you must live it and learn it in all facets of life. Through it all Christian has been inducted into several major honor societies since attending middle school and high school. Christian is goal-oriented and focused, as well as determined to do what is needed to get the job done that's asked of him.

He's played numerous sports, including football, basketball, baseball, and soccer, but narrowed his choice to track and field. One of his exceptional character traits is his leadership qualities; he never has to be told twice to do something, and he never quits the job unless it's completed. His work ethic is great because he's totally intoned to what he's doing. Christian is a 12-time track and field AAU / High School All-American, 8-time AAU/USATF- Olympic Medalist with 11AAU National Indoor Medals, and has over 280 medals in total. Christian received two Maryland Governors Citation and two Senate Citations for track and field and was featured in the Maryland Independent Newspaper four times. He was also named AAU Track and Field Most Outstanding

Runner for 2018. On his high school varsity track team at Westlake High School in Waldorf, Maryland, Christian was the only freshman on both 4X100M and 4X200M, which went on to come in 2nd & 3rd in the 2A in the State of Maryland, respectively. In his high school 2024 indoor track season, he amassed huge achievements, starting off with me making it to the SMAC championships in the 55M & 4X200m relay, in which he ran 3rd leg, which helped his team make it to the finals in both and his relay team winning gold, which also made it to the regionals in the 55M & 4X200m relay again making it to the finals in both and his relay team winning gold, then making it to the MD 2A state championships in both with his 4X200m relay team winning the state championships and finally Christian and his 4X200m relay team qualified for the Adidas Nationals Championship Division and he qualified in the 60m and posted a 7.11 for his first time ever running the 60m in high school. His 4X200m relay team posted a 127.76, taking 3rd place overall in becoming US #9, MD public schools #1, and all MD schools # 3 behind Carroll and Bullis, the two most dominant schools in the country. Christian's high school won the 2024 Maryland 2A State Championship. Both relay teams he was on came in first place and got gold medals as well as breaking meet and state records. Christian became a 3 Time Adidas National track and field All-American in the Nationals as well and had several colleges reaching out to him because of his accomplishments and achievements.

Christian truly believes in development, so he trains a lot by myself to develop and sharpen his skills. Christian strives to be the best version of himself and, without a doubt, a team player. He sacrifices what's needed for his team to win. With these characteristics and traits these attributes would make Christian a great fit for any College and any track team. What stands out the most in his achievements is that Christian is a Principal's honor roll student and boasts a 4.5 GPA in school!!!!! This is resilience in every respect of the word.

SOUTHERN MARYLAND NEWS

Westlake boys win 2A state track and field title

Ted Black tblack@somdnews.com May 24, 2024

3 of 4

Westlake High School junior Christian Wilbon breaks from the starting blocks in the boys' 400-meter relay last week at the Maryland 2A state track and field championships at the Prince George's Sports & Learning Complex. The Wolverines won that event (41.37) and also attained 73 points to capture the state team title on May 23.

TED BLACK/Southern Maryland News

MARYLAND
ATHLETIC ASSOCIATION

CHRISTIAN WILBON WITH THE 2024 2A MARYLAND STATE CHAMPIONSHIP TRACK AND FIELD TROPHY

CHRISTIAN WILBON 3-TIME 2023-2024 INDOOR AND OUTDOOR ADIDAS NATIONALS ALL-AMERICAN

CHAPTER 5

T—TRIUMPH

As Coach Dr. Wilbon looks back on the journey of his life, he's struck by the multitude of triumphs and victories that have shaped his path. From the earliest days of his humble beginnings to the pinnacle of his achievements in education, sports, and coaching, each triumph stands as a testament to his unwavering resilience and unyielding determination.

Growing up amidst the hustle and bustle of Washington, DC, Coach Dr. Wilbon encountered his fair share of obstacles and challenges. Yet, he steadfastly refused to let his circumstances dictate his destiny. Instead, he embraced education as a beacon of hope—a pathway to a brighter future. Coach Dr. Wilbon poured his heart and soul into his studies, viewing each academic milestone as a hard-earned triumph. Whether it was acing a difficult test or graduating with honors, every accomplishment reinforced his belief in the transformative power of education to uplift and empower lives.

From the bustling streets of his hometown to the echoing courts of basketball arenas, Dr. Wilbon's journey was marked by his love for sports. Basketball, in particular, captured his passion from an early age, becoming a source of joy, challenge, and triumph. As he dribbled and shot his way through countless games and tournaments, Coach Dr. Wilbon experienced the exhilarating highs of victory and the humbling lows of defeat. Yet, with each game, he learned valuable lessons about perseverance, teamwork, and the resilience of the human spirit.

Transitioning from player to coach was a natural evolution for Dr. Wilbon—one that opened up new avenues for triumph and success. Guiding young athletes to victory became not just a profession but a calling—a source of deep fulfillment and purpose. Winning championships as a coach was a dream realized, but more than the shiny trophies and accolades, it was the relationships forged with his players that left an indelible mark on Dr. Wilbon's heart.

Through it all, Dr. Wilbon's journey has been a testament to the power of resilience and determination. Each triumph, no matter how small, has contributed to the mosaic of his life, shaping him into the person he is today. As he continues to navigate the twists and turns of his journey, Coach Dr. Wilbon carries with him the knowledge that with passion, perseverance, and a belief in oneself, anything is possible.

One of the most profound moments in Dr. Wilbon's life was the day he received his first college degree. It wasn't just a piece of paper—it was a culmination of years of relentless effort and countless sacrifices. As he strode across the stage to accept his diploma, a rush of emotions flooded over him. Pride, accomplishment, and a sense of fulfillment washed over him like a warm wave. It was a moment that he had dreamed of working for, and now, it was a reality.

Earning that degree wasn't just a personal victory for Dr. Wilbon; it was a symbol of the beginning of a new chapter in his life. It signified the start of a journey filled with boundless opportunities and endless possibilities. Armed with his newfound knowledge and credentials, Coach Dr. Wilbon embarked on a path paved with promise and potential.

However, Coach Dr. Wilbon's thirst for knowledge and passion for personal growth knew no bounds. Fueled by a relentless drive to excel, he continued to pursue higher education, earning multiple degrees in various fields. Each degree was more than just an academic achievement—it was a triumph of dedication, perseverance, and an unwavering commitment to self-improvement.

With each new degree under his belt, Dr. Wilbon's horizons expanded, and his capabilities grew. He gained invaluable skills and knowledge that would prove instrumental in shaping his future endeavors. From business administration to psychology, each field of study offered Coach Dr. Wilbon new perspectives and insights, enriching his understanding of the world and equipping him with the tools needed to navigate life's challenges.

Through his pursuit of higher education, Coach Dr. Wilbon not only broadened his intellectual horizons but also set a shining example for others to follow. His relentless pursuit of knowledge and unwavering dedication to personal growth serve as a testament to the transformative power of education. Dr. Wilbon's journey is a reminder that with passion, perseverance, and a thirst for learning, anything is possible.

Beyond his academic pursuits, Coach Dr. Wilbon found another realm of success that resonated deeply with him: sports, particularly basketball. From a tender age, the sport captured his heart, igniting a passion that would burn brightly throughout his life. Coach Dr. Wilbon devoted countless hours to refining his skills on the court, practicing tirelessly to hone his craft. As a player, he experienced the exhilarating highs of victory and the crushing lows of defeat. Yet, with each game, Coach Dr. Wilbon embraced the opportunity for growth and learning, recognizing that both triumphs and setbacks were essential steps on the path to mastery.

Transitioning from player to coach was a natural evolution for Dr. Wilbon—one that opened up a new chapter of triumphs and successes. Guiding young athletes to victory became not just a profession but a calling—a source of profound joy and fulfillment. Winning championships as a coach was undoubtedly a crowning achievement, but for Dr. Wilbon, the true reward lay in the relationships he forged with his players.

Each victory on the court was a testament to Dr. Wilbon's leadership and guidance, but it was the bonds of camaraderie and trust that he built with his team that meant the most to him. Through his coaching, Coach Dr. Wilbon not only imparted knowledge and skills but also instilled in his players the values of teamwork, perseverance, and integrity. Together, they celebrated triumphs, weathered setbacks, and forged lifelong memories that transcended the boundaries of the basketball court.

For Dr. Wilbon, success in sports wasn't just about winning games or earning accolades—it was about making a positive impact on the lives of others. Through his dedication to coaching, he inspired and empowered countless young athletes to reach their full potential, both on and off the court. In doing so, Coach Dr. Wilbon found his own sense of purpose and fulfillment, affirming that true triumph lies not in personal achievements but in the ability to uplift and empower others.

As a mentor, Coach Dr. Wilbon cherished the opportunity to guide and nurture young athletes, both on and off the court. It was a privilege he held dear, witnessing firsthand the transformation and growth of these individuals. Seeing them evolve into confident, skilled players brought Coach Dr. Wilbon immense satisfaction and joy. Their triumphs became his own as he reveled in their successes and celebrated their achievements.

For Dr. Wilbon, being a mentor was more than just imparting knowledge and skills—it was about instilling values and fostering personal growth. He took pride in not only helping his mentees excel in their athletic endeavors but also in shaping them into well-rounded individuals with strong character and integrity.

Reflecting on his journey, Coach Dr. Wilbon is filled with gratitude for the triumphs and successes that have dotted his path. Each victory, whether big or small, has left an indelible mark on his life, shaping him into the person he is today. Through the highs and lows, Coach Dr. Wilbon has learned invaluable lessons about resilience, perseverance, and the unwavering belief in oneself.

As he continues to pursue his goals and aspirations, Coach Dr. Wilbon carries with him the wisdom gleaned from his experiences. He knows that with passion, determination, and a steadfast belief in one's own potential, there are no limits to what can be achieved. Dr. Wilbon's journey serves as a testament to the transformative power of perseverance and the profound impact that belief in oneself can have on shaping one's destiny.

CHAPTER 6

S – SUCCESS

In the unfolding story of his life, Coach Dr. Wilbon stands at a pivotal moment, ready to delve into the intricate layers of success and its profound implications. As he looks back upon the chapters of his past, he discerns a rich tapestry woven with triumphs, setbacks, and moments of profound growth that have shaped his understanding of success. With each memory revisited, Coach Dr. Wilbon embarks on a journey of introspection, unraveling the essence of success and its significance in both the realm of sports and the broader canvas of life.

Born and bred amidst the vibrant streets of urban Washington, DC, Dr. Wilbon's journey epitomized resilience, determination, and an unwavering dedication to excellence. From his earliest days, he was drawn to the allure of sports, particularly basketball, which ignited a fervent passion within his soul. It was on the sun-drenched courts of his neighborhood that Coach Dr. Wilbon first tasted the intoxicating elixir of success, savoring the exhilarating highs of victory and weathering the humbling lows of defeat. Yet, with each game played and every challenge faced, he gleaned invaluable lessons about the power of perseverance, the importance of teamwork, and the unwavering pursuit of greatness.

As Coach Dr. Wilbon reflects on his journey, he realizes that success is not merely about winning games or achieving goals—it is a journey of self-discovery and personal growth. It is about embracing the journey with resilience, determination, and an unwavering belief in oneself. Through the highs and lows, Coach Dr. Wilbon learned to navigate the twists and turns of life's unpredictable terrain, emerging stronger and more resilient with each trial faced.

The bustling streets of Washington, DC, served as the backdrop for Dr. Wilbon's formative years, shaping his character and instilling in him a fierce sense of determination. Despite the myriad challenges that surrounded him, Coach Dr. Wilbon remained steadfast in his pursuit of excellence, refusing to be deterred by obstacles in his path. It was this indomitable spirit that propelled him forward, driving him to surpass his own limitations and reach for the stars.

On the basketball court, Coach Dr. Wilbon discovered not only a passion but also a profound sense of purpose. It was here that he honed his skills, forged lifelong friendships, and experienced the euphoria of victory and the sting of defeat. Each game served as a crucible of learning, teaching Coach Dr. Wilbon invaluable lessons about resilience, perseverance, and the importance of never giving up, no matter the odds.

In the realm of coaching, Coach Dr. Wilbon found a new avenue for success—a platform from which he could inspire and empower the next generation of athletes. Guiding young players to victory became not just a profession but a calling—a sacred duty to nurture and cultivate the potential within each individual. Through coaching, Coach Dr. Wilbon discovered a profound sense of fulfillment in witnessing the growth and development of his players, celebrating their triumphs as his own, and finding purpose in making a positive impact on their lives.

Transitioning from player to coach marked a significant milestone in Dr. Wilbon's journey—an organic progression that unlocked new realms of opportunity and personal growth. Guiding young athletes to victory ceased to be merely a profession; it became a profound calling—a sacred responsibility to nurture and empower the next generation of champions. Through coaching, Coach Dr. Wilbon discovered a profound sense of fulfillment in witnessing the triumphs of his players. Each victory celebrated by his team felt like a personal achievement, and he derived profound satisfaction from witnessing their growth and development both on and off the court.

In the realm of mentorship, Coach Dr. Wilbon unearthed yet another avenue for success—a pathway illuminated by empathy, guidance, and unwavering support. As a mentor, he was bestowed with the privilege of shepherding young athletes on their journey to greatness. Instilling in them the values of discipline, perseverance, and integrity became not just a duty but a labor of love. Coach Dr. Wilbon wholeheartedly embraced this role, finding fulfillment in the knowledge that he was making a positive impact on the lives of others. Each mentee's success served as a testament to the power of mentorship and reaffirmed Dr. Wilbon's belief in the transformative potential of guidance and support.

As Coach Dr. Wilbon pauses to reflect on the path he has traveled, he delves into the essence of success—a notion that extends far beyond tangible rewards and external recognition. In his contemplation, he discerns that success is a multifaceted journey, comprising not only material achievements but also personal growth, fulfillment, and the lasting impact one leaves on others. To Coach Dr. Wilbon, true success encompasses a harmonious balance of these elements, intertwining them into a tapestry of purpose and meaning.

For Dr. Wilbon, success transcends the mere attainment of goals or victories on the playing field. It encompasses the cultivation of inner strength, resilience, and perseverance—the qualities that fortify one's spirit in the face of adversity. Moreover, success is about embodying integrity and upholding moral values in all facets of life, regardless of the challenges encountered along the way.

In essence, success is a journey of self-discovery and self-actualization—a continuous evolution toward becoming the best version of oneself. It is about striving for excellence in every endeavor, embracing growth, and making a positive difference in the lives of others. Dr. Wilbon's reflection underscores the transformative power of success—a force that transcends individual accomplishments and resonates deeply with the human spirit.

At the core of Dr. Wilbon's philosophy of success lies a fundamental principle: the importance of setting clear goals and relentlessly pursuing them. For Dr. Wilbon, success is not merely a destination to reach but a continuous journey—a perpetual striving for excellence fueled by passion, determination, and an unshakeable belief in oneself. Drawing from his own life experiences and keen observations, Coach Dr. Wilbon imparts invaluable strategies for achieving success, particularly in the realms of coaching and mentorship.

Effective communication stands as a cornerstone of Dr. Wilbon's approach to success. He emphasizes the significance of clear and open lines of communication, both within teams and between mentors and mentees. By fostering an environment where ideas can flow freely, and feedback is welcomed, Coach Dr. Wilbon believes that athletes and mentees can thrive and reach their fullest potential.

Furthermore, Coach Dr. Wilbon underscores the indispensable role of perseverance, resilience, and continuous learning in the pursuit of success. He encourages readers to view failure not as a setback but as a stepping stone to growth and development. By embracing setbacks as opportunities for learning and improvement, individuals can cultivate resilience and bounce back stronger than before.

In Dr. Wilbon's view, success is not solely defined by external achievements or accolades but by the personal growth and fulfillment attained along the way. He emphasizes the importance of remaining humble, grateful, and focused on the journey itself rather than fixating solely on the end result. By maintaining a mindset of gratitude and a willingness to learn from both successes and failures, individuals can unlock their full potential and achieve greatness in all aspects of life.

Ultimately, Dr. Wilbon's philosophy of success serves as a beacon of inspiration, guiding readers toward a path of self-discovery, growth, and achievement. Through effective goal-setting, unwavering determination, and a commitment to continuous learning, individuals can embark on a journey of success that transcends boundaries and unlocks boundless possibilities for personal and professional fulfillment.

CHAPTER 7

GAME CHANGER

In the vast expanse of sports coaching history, Dr. Wilbon's story emerges as a testament to innovation and adaptability. His journey is characterized by an unwavering pursuit of excellence and a dedication to challenging the norms of conventional wisdom. As Coach Dr. Wilbon reflects on his evolution as a coach, he finds himself navigating the ever-changing landscape of sports coaching with determination and resilience.

From the very beginning of his coaching career, Coach Dr. Wilbon recognized the potential for innovation to revolutionize the field of sports coaching. Driven by a fervent desire to unlock the full potential of his athletes, he embarked on a journey of exploration, constantly seeking new methods to enhance performance and optimize training techniques. Drawing from his own experiences and keen observations, Coach Dr. Wilbon shares insights into the pivotal role that innovation has played in shaping his coaching philosophy and approach.

Throughout his career, Coach Dr. Wilbon has been at the forefront of implementing innovative strategies and techniques to propel his athletes to greater heights. Whether it's integrating cutting-edge technology into training regimens or pioneering novel approaches to player development, Coach Dr. Wilbon has consistently pushed the boundaries of traditional coaching practices. By embracing innovation, he has been able to stay ahead of the curve and deliver exceptional results for his athletes.

Moreover, Dr. Wilbon's commitment to innovation extends beyond the realm of technology. He recognizes the importance of fostering a culture of creativity and openness within his coaching staff and athletes. By encouraging experimentation and embracing new ideas, Coach Dr. Wilbon has created an environment where innovation flourishes, and athletes are empowered to reach their full potential.

As Coach Dr. Wilbon reflects on his journey, he emphasizes the transformative power of innovation in sports coaching. It is not merely about adopting new technologies or techniques but about embracing a mindset of continual improvement and adaptation. By remaining open to change and willing to explore new possibilities, coaches can unlock new levels of success and make a lasting impact on the world of sports coaching.

With the rise of technology, a new dawn emerged in the realm of sports coaching, presenting Coach Dr. Wilbon with a plethora of opportunities to revolutionize athlete performance. Embracing this transformative potential with fervor, Coach Dr. Wilbon swiftly integrated various technological tools into his coaching arsenal. From sophisticated video analysis software to cutting-edge data tracking tools, technology became an indispensable ally in Dr.

Wilbon's mission to elevate athlete performance to unprecedented levels. Delving into the nuances of technology in coaching, Coach Dr. Wilbon sheds light on how coaches can leverage these tools to delve deeper into athlete performance metrics, refine training methodologies, and foster a culture of continuous improvement.

Beyond technological innovations, Coach Dr. Wilbon delves into the realm of novel methodologies and approaches that have reshaped conventional coaching practices. As the coaching landscape evolves, coaches are continually pushing the boundaries of traditional methods to unlock new realms of athlete potential. Coach Dr. Wilbon shares firsthand examples of how he has embraced these innovative approaches in his coaching journey, demonstrating how he has integrated cutting-edge training techniques and pioneering player development strategies into his coaching repertoire. By embracing innovation, Coach Dr. Wilbon has not only propelled himself to new heights of success but has also empowered his athletes to achieve unparalleled levels of performance.

Reflecting on his journey as a trailblazer in the realm of coaching, Coach Dr. Wilbon underscores the paramount importance of adaptability and open-mindedness in navigating the ever-evolving landscape of sports coaching. In an environment characterized by rapid change and innovation, success hinges upon one's ability to embrace new ideas, challenge traditional norms, and think creatively. Drawing from his wealth of experiences, Coach Dr. Wilbon imparts invaluable insights and personal anecdotes, urging readers to cultivate a mindset of flexibility and resilience in their coaching endeavors.

Moreover, Coach Dr. Wilbon highlights the transformative potential of innovation in driving positive change within the realm of sports coaching. By embracing change and harnessing emerging technologies and methodologies, coaches can unlock unprecedented opportunities for growth and success. Coach Dr. Wilbon emphasizes the need for coaches to remain proactive in their pursuit of innovation, leveraging advancements in technology and adopting progressive coaching approaches to enhance athlete performance and achieve optimal results.

As Coach Dr. Wilbon delves deeper into the topic, he underscores the importance of continuous learning and self-improvement in the pursuit of innovation. In a rapidly evolving field, it is essential for coaches to remain abreast of the latest developments and trends, constantly seeking out new knowledge and skills to enhance their coaching practices. Coach Dr. Wilbon encourages coaches to adopt a growth mindset, viewing challenges as opportunities for learning and growth rather than obstacles to be overcome.

Furthermore, Coach Dr. Wilbon emphasizes the role of collaboration and knowledge sharing in fostering innovation within the coaching community. By exchanging ideas and best practices with fellow coaches, individuals can gain new perspectives and insights, fueling creativity and innovation in their coaching endeavors. Coach Dr. Wilbon encourages coaches to cultivate a supportive and collaborative environment where ideas are freely exchanged and collective wisdom is leveraged to drive positive change and elevate the standards of sports coaching.

Coach Dr. Wilbon's reflections on the importance of adaptability, open-mindedness, and innovation serve as a guiding light for coaches seeking to excel in their craft. By embracing change, fostering a culture of continuous learning, and leveraging emerging technologies and methodologies, coaches can position themselves at the forefront of innovation in the field, driving continuous improvement and excellence in athlete performance.

Coach Dr. Wilbon's journey as a revolutionary figure in sports coaching epitomizes the profound impact of innovation and adaptability. His experiences and insights serve as a beacon of inspiration for readers, encouraging them to embrace change and break free from the constraints of conventional thinking. Dr. Wilbon's narrative underscores the importance of challenging the status quo and continually striving for excellence in coaching practices. By following in Dr. Wilbon's footsteps, readers can empower themselves to navigate the dynamic landscape of sports coaching with confidence, unlocking new opportunities for success and growth for both themselves and their athletes. Ultimately, Dr. Wilbon's journey serves as a testament to the transformative power of innovation, adaptability, and a relentless pursuit of excellence in the field of sports coaching.

COACH DR. WILBON / 2024 4X100M ADIDAS ALL-AMERICANS / CHRISTIAN WILBON, KENDALL TYSON, EBUBE EMECHEBE, DAVID NNABUKO

COACH DR. WILBON WITH HIS TEAM THE LAKE TC / 4X2OOM / 2024 OUTDOOR ADIDAS ALL-AMERICANS

CHRISTIAN WILBON, EBUBE EMECHEBE, KELECHI ANYANWU, AND DAVID NNABUKO

Westlake High School under / Xceleration Nation 2023-2024 Indoor Adidas Nationals All-Americans / Christian Wilbon, Kendall Tyson, Ebube Emechebe, David Nnabuko

Dedication:

I would like to dedicate this book to all of the USA athletes that competed in the 2024 Paris Olympics!!! S.P.O.R.T.S. identifies everything that you stand for and have achieved in your lives!!!

Coach Dr. Kevin Wilbon Sr.

Made in the USA
Columbia, SC
08 August 2024

40187733R00048